Tom's New Pet

Story by Diane DeFord

Illustrations by E. Silas Smith

🎔 Dominie Press, Inc.

Tom ran ahead of his sister, Sally, and his dad. He was too excited to wait any longer. He ran into the pet shop to find a new pet.

First Tom went to look at the turtles. He held one in his hand. He stroked its hard shell. The turtle just looked at him.

"Don't you want a turtle for a pet?" asked Sally.

"No," said Tom. "Not a turtle."

Tom watched the fish swimming in the fish tank. He put his hand on the glass. It was cold. His dad said, "Fish are easy to take care of. Don't you want some fish?"

"No," said Tom. "No fish."

Then Tom saw a big snake. He ran over
to look. It was coiled at the bottom of a tank.
Sally said, "You don't want a snake for a pet."

"Why not?" asked Tom.

"Mom is scared of snakes," she said.

"No, then I don't want a snake," said Tom.

Tom touched the lizards. They felt smooth but very cold. His dad shook his head. Sally stood on the other side of the room, shaking her head from side to side.

6

Tom looked at the kittens. But his friend Andy had a cat, and Tom wanted something very different.

So Tom looked at the puppies. But his friend Pat had a dog.

So Tom looked at the frogs. But Sally made a face when he looked at the frogs.

"No, no frogs," Tom thought.

Tom looked at the birds in their cages,
but when he put his finger between the bars,
the parrot bit him.

8

When Tom ran over to the mice, Sally pulled him away. "No mice," she said.

Just for fun, Tom picked up a cricket.

"No crickets," said his dad.

Sally found a chair she could sit on. She pulled out some cards from her pocket to practice a magic trick.

Tom's dad sighed. "You've seen EVERYTHING this store has in the way of pets," he said. "Now what?"

Tom looked all around the room again.
Turtles, snakes, frogs, fish, and lizards were too cold.

Birds, crickets, mice, kittens, and dogs were
just okay, but not quite right.

14

Then Tom ran over to the store window. Hopping around inside a fence were some baby rabbits. "This is it!" he said. "I want a rabbit!"

Sally and his dad shrugged.

"Why a rabbit?" Sally asked.

Tom laughed. "It's not too big, and not too small. It's just right!" he said.

Publisher: Raymond Yuen
Consultant: Adria F. Klein
Editor: Bob Rowland
Designer: Natalie Chupil
Illustrator: E. Silas Smith

Published by:

🌀 **Dominie Press, Inc.**

1949 Kellogg Avenue
Carlsbad, California 92008 USA

www.dominie.com

ISBN 0-7685-0643-3

Printed in Singapore by PH Productions Pte Ltd

3 4 5 6 PH 02

ITP